Picture a table covered with

all that matters to you.

The light seems bluer here, your thoughts are

clear and solid.

This is where you make

sense of things.

You have your own categories and theories

charted on this table.

Each element in your world

has a definite life and voice.

You have a definite life and voice.

This is the Table of Everything.

For Rob, Rory and rocks

First published in 2000
by Allen & Unwin
9 Atchison Street
St Leonards, NSW 1590
Australia
Phone: (61 2) 8425 0100
Fax: (61 2) 9906 2218
E-mail: frontdesk@allen-unwin.com.au
Web: http://www.allen-unwin.com.au

National Library of Australia
Cataloguing-in-Publication Entry:
White, Trudy.
Table of Everything.

ISBN 1 86508 135 3.

1. Life-Fiction. I Title.

A823.3

Designed by Trudy White and Tom Sapountsis
Typeset by Tom Sapountsis
Printed in Australia by Australian Print Group

1 3 5 7 9 10 8 6 4 2

Table of everything

Trudy White

ALLEN & UNWIN

Contents

Method of Living

On page 76 of *The Beekeeper's Handbook*, published in 1965, you can see the photograph of a young woman opening a three-deck hive without wearing a veil or gloves. She has dark hair pulled into a bun on top of her head. Several bees sit on her hairstyle like ornaments.

The purpose of that photograph was, I suppose, to demonstrate that you can safely handle bees without protective clothing, if you know what you are doing.

I think the photograph influenced me in such a way that from the day I first saw it I started to go about things as if I was inspecting a hive with bare hands: gently smoking the entrance; waiting a little; puffing smoke under the lid; whacking the lid firmly on the ground; taking the second frame out. A definite sense of what was to be done, how and in what order. I think I felt some security would come from a set routine and method of living. I decided to apply this to myself for a year, as a trial, and continue if it proved successful.

First, I set my house up as follows:

two tables—one for work to do later, one for work to do now;

a rack of clothes divided into work, leisure and special engagements wear;

a bookshelf placed behind my bedhead so I could reach out and select a book without leaving my bed;

notepad and pen attached by string to the bedhead in case of any brilliant middle-of-the-night ideas;

notepad and pen attached by string to the stove in case of any sumptuous middle-of-cooking-dinner ideas;

notepad and pen attached by string to every chair in the house in case of any urgent middle-of-sitting-down ideas.

Then I trained the dog to collect the paper, which would be thrown into the yard at five minutes past six, and wake me up with it opened to the weather report.

I tried to teach him to open the curtains, but he wouldn't. So I resorted to rigging up a pulley and rope to open them myself from the bed. I decided against teaching him to make me a cup of tea.

So, I started the day with a perfect arrangement.

After reading for half an hour, I would sit up and decide what to wear. If it was a day beginning with M or W, I would dress in a white shirt, black trousers or skirt and stockings, brush my hair, count the number of hairs left on the brush, log this in a pad kept in the bathroom, pat the dog and leave the house without breakfast.

A day beginning with T, F or S would begin the same way except that I would read the paper, then a chapter of my book. I'd dress in something comfortable, depending on the weather and what sort of mood I was in. I'd comb my hair with my fingers, and the dog and I would stroll together along the road to the park, buying a loaf of bread on the way.

I'd have my brown leather satchel with work equipment: notebook, pencils, pens, magnifying glass, plant identification book, bird call book, rock and stone identification book, all set and ready to use.

Usually we'd sit across from the river and the dog would run around for a bit, then sit a few metres away from me. I would pick a spot away from signs of people and settle for a while. I'd sit there for up to an hour, or try to. Sometimes I'd stretch my arms and legs a bit. Mainly I'd sit still, though, and look generally at the colours of things, the shapes, the reflections in the water, or listen to the sounds of birds, cars, falling sticks.

It would be a fight to get through the first stages of restless-mind, then I'd reach a place where I could be content to sit and look at things and be still and not think. Because when you are thinking you are not looking, and I needed to be very focused.

I decided to train myself to memorise the details of things: the texture of a granite rock, the call of a wattle bird, a few things each day. I would record them in my notebook and check up the next time to see if I'd missed anything. Like the sparkling of tiny rock particles in the sunlight.

I tried not to reason why I was doing this activity. I just knew it would be useful. I'd write a weather report at the top of the page then revise the past few days' observations.

Then I'd pick a new thing to look at. I didn't have a set method for choosing something, but usually it'd go: plant (separate parts in detail); rock (individual form); animal or insect (movement or sound); cloud type (shape); and with everything I'd note its colour, smell, feel, approximate age, whereabouts, name, aim in life and size. I'd do this for a few hours and by then it'd be about noon and the dog would nuzzle me to start walking again.

We'd walk to a spot on the top of a hill where we could see the city buildings in the distance, all squashed together. I'd tear off a piece of bread for the dog and one for me, and I'd think about who was in those buildings looking out at the parklands and did they look out much. I'd sit there and draw for a bit and write notes, sometimes imagining the lives of people in the buildings, but mostly I was more interested in what colours the buildings were and how such heavy structures were made to stay upright.

By the time we returned home, we'd be ready to do some work. The dog would go outside and dig up his bones, and I'd sit at my table of work to do now and try to dig up some bones of my own.

Because this was the worst part: I was so organised I could never do any actual work.

After the year was up, I evaluated the pros and cons of the organised method of living:

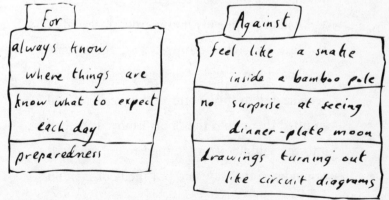

For
always know where things are
know what to expect each day
preparedness

Against
feel like a snake inside a bamboo pole
no surprise at seeing dinner-plate moon
drawings turning out like circuit diagrams

So, I took on the disorganised method of living to see if it would offer me more creative freedom and inspire me to do some proper work.

To get into the mood of disorganised and wildly creative living, I took as my model a picture from a book called *Disasters of Nature*. It was an aerial photograph of a house with the roof blown off by a freak wind.

Looking at that picture made you feel like you wanted to throw up and run a marathon and eat the biggest bowl of spaghetti in the world, simultaneously. I roughly tore it out of the book and taped it to the wall of my room with masking tape that would be sure to dry out and peel off soon enough.

I had to change my house around, get rid of all those organised things, so I took some cardboard boxes full of newspapers that I had been saving to throw out on the weekend and emptied them onto the floor. I moved the bed into the middle of my lounge room, where it would be in the way, and put the bookshelf on top of the bed so that when I wanted to sleep I would have to move it. I took all the books out first, of course, and messed up their categories and piled them in a corner.

By replacing the thick curtains in the lounge room with gladwrap, I would be sure to sleep fitfully and dream rich and disturbing pantomimes.

I put the dog's bed on one table, turning it from the table of things to be done now into the table of dog's bed. The other table, the table of things to be done later, stayed as it was, because I figured that is the first thing to do if you want to become disorganised: put everything off until tomorrow.

Then I smashed up all the matching, pristine-white crockery I had bought the year before and strewed the pieces over the garden, replacing them with some odd, cracked, used cups from the op-shop. Then I removed the strawberry-patch bird-netting, and dug up the dog's bones and brought them inside, which thoroughly confused the dog.

Next, I had to disrupt my morning routine. I cancelled the newspaper and pulled apart all the notebooks with string and hid them around the house. I closed my eyes and threw my keys into the garden. I jumbled up my clothes.

Now, when I woke up in the afternoon, I would dress in a white shirt, tie, mismatched socks and sneakers, and head over to the park, forgetting my books and pens. The dog picked up on the theme and ran away a lot. I would sit at a random spot and stare blankly at something or other, thinking all the time about what I was doing tomorrow or what I had been doing the day before. Often I'd wish I had something to eat in my pocket.

Sometimes I'd recreate the plot of a movie that I couldn't quite remember, replacing parts with scenes from my own life, or stories somebody had told me. Or I'd go over a horrible event that had occurred in the past and get all worked up about it until I couldn't help myself —I had to think about it again and again and feel old hurts opening up. Then I'd lie down and sleep for a while; I never knew how long, since my watch had stopped.

So I prevented myself from observing the scenery, except in breaks between thoughts.

I soon got bored and returned home, climbing in the bathroom window because I still hadn't found my keys (actually, I hadn't looked for them). I would eat an out-of-season piece of fruit, or some suspect cheese. I sat at my table of things to do later and stared at the piles of papers layered with dirty plates, like very crunchy filo pastry.

This went on for about a year, with even more dispiriting results as far as my work was concerned.

One day I was picking up crusts and books off the floor when a book fell open before me: *How To Rebuild Your Car Engine In Ten Easy Lessons*. The page showed a picture of an engine, cut away to show all the working parts, like an X-ray photograph.

That's it, I thought. This year I dedicate to living as if my life is an X-ray machine! And the dog and I went out to buy some equipment.

Sunrise Conversation

Let's get up at 4.30 tomorrow morning and
walk to the park for sunrise.

No, let's get up at 3.30 and drive out to the
beach for sunrise.

OK. Let's get up at 3.30, drive out to the
beach for sunrise and eat peanut butter
sandwiches in the sand dunes.

Hey, let's go out to the beach for sunrise and
sit in the sand dunes eating peanut butter
sandwiches and drinking champagne.

Let's pack champagne, peanut butter sandwiches and chocolate, miso soup and coffee,
drive out to the beach for sunrise and sit in
the sand dunes.

Let's take sleeping-bags to sit in.

Why don't we take sleeping-bags to sit in, go
to the sand dunes, unpack everything, sit in
the sleeping-bags and watch the sunrise?

Actually, we could pack the champagne,
peanut butter sandwiches, chocolate, miso soup
and coffee in the sleeping-bags, so it's easier
to carry over the sand dunes in the dark while
we find our position for sunrise.

We're going to need torches.

Why don't we pack the car and leave now for the beach, carry our stuff in the sleeping-bags over the sand dunes by torchlight, find a spot, unpack everything, hop in the sleeping-bags and go to sleep, wait for sunrise and wake up when we're already there?

I know, we could eat the food now!

Hang on, if we pack the car tonight, drive out to the beach and set up ready for sunrise, we might not wake up in time.

Why don't we pack the car and drive east, and just keep driving until we see the sunrise?

Look, why don't we pack everything in the house into cardboard boxes and bury it in the back-yard, take the sleeping-bags and essential gear, leave now for sunrise, head east, keep driving until we come to the edge of the land, unpack and sit in the sleeping-bags drinking miso soup, turn the car into a boat and sail around the world always looking for sunrise?

Oh no, I'm working tomorrow! We'll have to wait until the weekend.

Poetry Ambush

Last Wednesday night, when I went to call the cat in, he took longer than usual. I had already turned my back to the cold air and only paid a wink of attention to his miaow, which sounded more like a faint:

"Yesternight the sun went hence"

I am not a man given to fanciful imaginings, yet I was overly tired, and my mind, being occupied with such boring tasks during a working day, strains to break its tether after dark. I gave the matter no further thought.

The following morning, I was running so late that my toast had to be bread, and my cup of tea a suck on a tea bag.

Bumping my briefcase into the laundry basket, I noticed the sleeping cat's tail sticking out. A muffled soprano voice arose, and said, I was certain:

> Drowning is not so pitiful
> As the attempt to rise

Had my mind been available for free thought that day, I would have searched it for clues.

As usual, I left the office as the sun began to set. It had been a bright day, and torn orange-pink tissue clouds striped the sky. Walking by the park, I started to think about the cat, now that I had allocated musing time, and this matter had arisen twice. He had been in my company for three years and never showed signs of being anything other than an ordinary feline. If he had a propensity for poetry, he didn't get it from me.

Along the path home, furry grey tree buds were beginning to swell, like miniature rabbits arranged on branches.

From the corner, I can see my house. Most of the garden is inaccessible to anything bigger than a dog, except for a tunnel through the plants to the door. It's overrun by plum trees pinkly blossoming, freshly open daffodils, a bee-plant grown to form a branchy cave. In the middle is a clearing where my cat was sitting on a mossy cushion, licking his paws in the fading sunlight.

I crept up to the open gate and went on all fours along the leafy tunnel. Holding my breath, I listened to his lilting feline voice recite, "On a Drop of Dew", by Andrew Marvell.

I crouched there through the whole poem:

See how the Orient Dew,
Shed from the Bosom of the Morn
Into the blowing Roses,
Yet careless of its Mansion new;
For the clear Region where twas born
Round in its self incloses.
And in its little Globes Extent,
Frames as it can its native Element.

The cat remembered every line, or else impro-
vised so well I could not pick it. To conclude,
he gave the poet's name and dates of living
(1621-1678), bowed elegantly and washed his
whiskers.

My kneecaps were concreting themselves to my legs from crouching, and my tie was caught on thorns, so I rolled onto my side and lay watching the last of the sun outline the leaves of the tunnel roof: ovate and obovate, rounded and rhomboidal, smooth and hairy, pendulous and spiked.

And the sunlight traced their forms across my skin.

Small Blue Windmill Painting

I know that I have to keep writing in order to keep writing, and meanwhile I'm dreaming of a small light-blue painting something like the one Tobie brought around and hung on the wall at Canning Street, before I knew her, before she moved in.

I remember thinking: I don't know if I like that painting, or even if it is much of a painting at all. It was small and crumbly-pale. As was my house. Which it suited.

Tobie stayed.

There was a windmill in the picture (and the blue and some red) and the windmill itself seemed to be more important than the painting of the windmill. That is, the *idea* of the windmill mattered more than how it appeared in the picture. A windmill's autograph.

Painted by Tobie some years before, the

picture was like marmalade made with fruit from the orange trees of a favourite grandmother who has since died. It exuded the aroma of significant memories.

One evening, when I was lying on the Battered Floral Chaise Longue (BFCL), I turned my head to the left to view the picture at close range. What was it about? What are you about?

Holland-bicycling, dewy-tent packing-up-of, old-ceramics—studio concentrating, long-drive—amusing windmill-counting, melted-chocolate hot-in-a-glass-drinking.

Everybody seeing BFCL at night called it beautiful and historic, and everybody seeing it in daylight said it needed to be pruned back to the roots.

I came home one day to find Tobie lying with her ear to BFCL's headrest, eyes closed, apparently listening.

Two-spoon Italian-film-watching, tuneless-earnest guitar-torture-of, stoner-ceiling-staring, thick-botanic-textbook breathing-in.

Tobie looked across to me then and I think some dust and blue paint particles from the windmill painting settled alongside some faded particles of maroon fibre from BFCL, and I knew that she would always be my friend.

Run by Ants

I wanted to improve my memory, so I went to
the library and took out a book all about it. The
author of *Lest You Forget* claimed to remember what underpants she wore on March the
thirteenth, 1985. This seemed a little extreme.
I figured I only wanted to remember
where I'd left my notebook, where I'd
left my car, and what was the secret
ingredient in Mum's vanilla custard,
so I just read every fourth page:

The information in your brain would fill
an encyclopedia ten billion pages long.
If you ripped out all the pages and laid
them end to end in a pathway from here
to the moon, you would not only be
exposing your thoughts to passers-by, it
would occupy you for ever.

As if I don't have enough to do! I went to page eight:

An example of someone with an extra-ordinary memory is Peter Bullerston, winner of the 1992 World Memory Championships. Bullerston is able to remember the exact order of 1,820 playing cards (35 packs).

For his own amusement, he has learned all 600 questions and answers from the board game *The Muppet Movie*.

To memorise the order of a list of unrelated items, Bullerston uses a technique called The Method of the Loci. He gives each playing card a character

(for example, the three of diamonds is a
man with a twirled moustache and very
long legs) and mentally places them
along a route he knows well.

His first route was a local golf course with
three landmarks at each of the eighteen
holes. So he thinks of a person with very
long legs stepping across a sand-bank
pursued by a green snake in a top hat,
heading for some wattle trees, and
remembers the cards: three of diamonds,
ace of hearts and king of clubs.

I don't know why I never thought of that. If
only I'd thought of my car as an apple tree and
the place I left it as a fold-up card table, I might
still be driving to the library.

I skipped through the book to page 20:

As recently uncovered by Positron
Emission Tomography (P.E.T.),

the human memory is a magnificent
apartment building run by sugar ants
(*Camponotus consobrinus*).

In this example, a piece of information
about ELEGANCE is greeted at the
miniature wrought-iron gates, and is
carried by a worker ant along the short-
term-memory corridor.

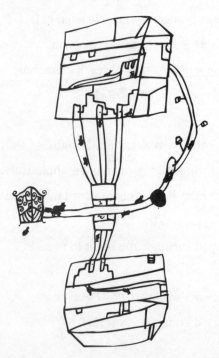

The ant creeps along the plush
green carpet for thirty seconds
before arriving at two doorways:
the episodic (personal) memory wing
and the semantic memory wing.

The worker ant must report first
to the reception desk where a
soldier worker will register the
information under a code and look
up in the card catalogue which

room it will go to. (Sometimes the
worker ant is given wrong
directions, and stores something
in an uncatalogued nook. This is
one explanation for amnesia.)

While the worker ant is waiting for instructions, it takes a number and goes into a basement fitted with stainless steel racks. Other worker ants help to place the information into a tiny glass bottle with a cork stopper. Some pieces of information need to be pickled in vinegar or dried by sulfuration.

This one is preserved in brandy and a label is stuck on.

When the ant's number is called, it takes the printed map in one clawed foot, the

bottle in the other, and hurries away.
This process takes a fraction of a second.
The ant takes the doorway to the
semantic memory wing in a sharp turn
and scuttles along on polished
floorboards, lit every so often by a
tasteful standard lamp. The hallway
branches at odd angles, like a tree pruned
by someone with new snippers.

The ant climbs tiny steps and weaves
through passages lined with doors,
each door numbered with brass digits,

some doors slightly ajar. The ant flashes
past a room lit by sparklers, a room wall-
papered in orange flowers, a room filled
with laminex tables. It stops outside the
door corresponding with its map:

ELEGANCE, REFINEMENT, GRACE etc.
Checks the numbers twice. The room it
enters is lined with smoked-glass
mirrors, a nest of tables in one corner.
The P.E.T. technology is not developed
quite enough to see what happens at this
stage, but we can deduce that the ant
gently places the bottle on an oak
sideboard of some kind, ready to be filed
by a more specialised ant.

Aha! So it wasn't my fault that I was too
preoccupied to memorise things! My ants were
below par. I would have to formulate a plan.
Either I could feed them up with sugary foods,
or I could replace them altogether.

I went for a walk around the block. (This is my favourite way of thinking.) On the way I bought a red icy-pole and a bag of lollies: sherbet bombs, buddies and licorice allsorts.

I started to have all sorts of thoughts while I chewed through them. The secret ingredient in Mum's vanilla custard is milk! My notebook is in my desk drawer! Around the next corner, I came across my car. Now I remembered, I had left it there after visiting the vet with our canary who had got his head stuck in my ant farm.

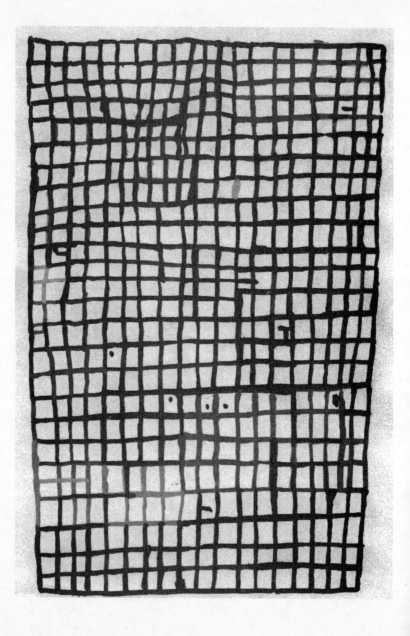

Pencil

Who, Brenda? She collects all kinds of pencils. Has done since she was three, apparently. She went to the Happy Hamburger Hut where they gave her a puzzle placemat and a grey lead pencil to draw with. Red outside with the H.H.H. motif on. As big as your little finger.

Oh yes, she could have gone the other way! Sometimes she talks about the beginnings of her collection, how things might have been if she'd taken the placemat home.

Now, when you go to Brenda's house, you'll see how neatly she stores them, all set out in that new extension. She's updating the data on them now with a grant from the government.

You can read the notes pasted on the glass cases,

but I can tell you some bits you won't read. There's her first box of coloured pencils on show, in a tin, with gold numbers on them. Well, she wouldn't let anyone else in Grade Four use them. At lunchtime, she would go back to the classroom, sneak open the tin and check they were still in order. We all dreamed of what we'd like to do with them.

She only drew sparingly, sensible pictures worthy of using up pencil for. Odd, the way

they've all been used up to the same length.
I don't know how she got through Grade Five,
myself.

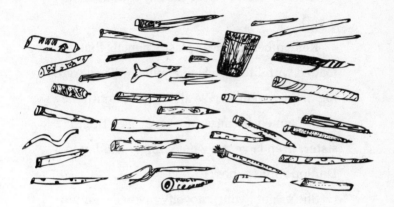

Then there's the pencil stub retrieved from
her baby sister's esophagus. You can imagine
Brenda throwing a fit so the surgeon would let
her keep it, can't you?

Make sure you get a good look at the pencil
used by Captain Cook to draw the first map of
Australia. She bought it at a Christies' auction
only recently. What do you mean, how do they
know?

Brenda's diversified her collection since she moved back here. She's got more than your classic old wood and grey-lead—I mean, graphite. (She would hate to hear me say that after this long.)

Remember the clear plastic pencils that you loaded with little leads like bullets? They were big in the seventies. We all had them until they were banned because of people like Brenda's sister. Brenda kept a whole range. Hidden in a Dunlop runners box.

She's got your novelty pencils—multi-coloured in the one stick (that's industry talk for pencil)—thick sticks, round sticks, a stick made from a branch, tiny coloured sticks, small as matches in a fairy pouch. Pencils from every country you could name.

They have led her into trouble, though. It takes a rare person to understand such a passion.

Her first boyfriend was a carpenter. She used to go on to me about his flat square pencil and chalk bag. I never thought it would last. I was happy for her when she met an architect who introduced her to silver mechanical pencils with built-in rubbers. But he diverted into computers and Brenda refused to update to mouses. That's why she's stayed single for so long.

When you get to the last cabinet at Brenda's, have a look at the bottom three shelves.

No, I won't tell you!

Oh, all right: her new husband's sharpener collection.

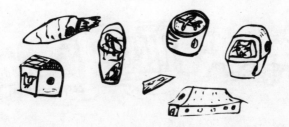

Very Slow Train

We decided the best thing to do with the money was either to buy a seventy-foot yacht and sail to Greece as we always planned, or buy an old train and restore it and start up a rail service that was the exact opposite of the one that ran between Melbourne and Sydney at the time, and make it spectacular, marvellous and affordable for families.

Given the factors, we went with the train plan. We like a bit of something to work on in our spare time.

We bought the oldest train we could find: ten cars long, solid wooden frame, leadlight upholstery, brass lamps, pressed tin windows. It had two dining cars, a caboose, five passenger carriages, four baggage cars, coal-fuelled engine with LPG conversion option, speed stripes, sick bags, pink tiled bathrooms, coloured glass lampshades like green tiger lilies, railway teapots, good guttering and new emergency brakes.

A grey man in Burwood sold it to us. He was wearing a fluoro safety jacket. He said the train had been sitting in his backyard for a hundred years, or thereabouts. He just tinkered on it. In a voice like breaking rocks he said it was a bit slow to get going, and any clunking would just be uneven tracks.

He threw in a couple of tonnes of coal at no extra charge. He said we could come back if we needed any train tracks later on.

With the money left over we set about our plans. Al wanted to do things methodically and draw designs first, but I wanted to rush in and dress up in one of the old train waitress uniforms and start nailing and painting.

Already, every room in our house was covered in large sheets of paper—the kitchen had all our maps with routes traced over, the lounge had car designs hiding the TV, the bed was somewhere underneath the third, fourth and fifth storey house plans. We ended up using a lot of these maps and plans anyway, in the final train design.

The first few carriages we wouldn't touch, apart from polishing the wood and shining up the leather seats. One dining car we also left pretty much as it was. It was the baggage cars that we were the most excited about. They were plain wooden rooms on wheels, ready to be transformed.

Al hired a big electric chainsaw and we sawed the top off a baggage car, making a tray car. Next we built a steel frame and put triple reinforced glass up to halfway, leaving the top open. This would be the fresh-air-and-scenery carriage. Already the train was the antithesis of any train in Australia at the time. Trains were heading the way of grocery shopping: becoming hygienised, plasticuled and de-friendlicated. They were getting faster and faster until the journey seemed incidental to the trip—it was over before you had a chance to open your newspaper or drink a cup of tea, if they offered tea at all.

We continued to make it the most fantastic train by installing couches facing outwards to the scenery. We placed little footstools in front of each couch, and a binoculars-holder either side.

So that people could bring their pets along for holidays, Al found some threadbare velvet armchairs for the dog customers, and wicker baskets for cats. There were also small cots for hamsters and other cavy travellers. Al thought people might want to bring along their reptiles, and we would have to separate the natural enemy animals to prevent chaos.

'Maybe we should have a policy of friendly animals,' I said. 'Like a test they sit to make sure there are no hiccups on the journey.'

Hiccups, droppings . . . we had to consider waste management.

I designed a toilet area for the animals that composted their poo, using tiger worms, and fed it through a tube to the on-board vegetable garden carriage. The garden was planted in the shape of Australia, with thyme state borders, lambs' lettuce to represent sheep farming areas and orange marigolds for Uluru. It would grow most of the plants used in cooking meals, and it would also provide pleasant surroundings for passengers who felt motion-sick from watching low-speed scenery passing.

My Aunt Ethel volunteered to work as chief cook. Ethel makes interesting plastic breadbag patchwork, but she wouldn't know a beetroot from a doorknob. And Al said we had too many doorknobs lying around to take the risk.

We employed Ethel as chief patchworker, because the roof was a bit rusted in parts.

Her husband, Bob, we thought would be a very useful person to have around. Bob makes wonderful sculptures by soldering nuts and bolts together, but he is also a specialist in cinema projection. He had hundreds of old film reels in his garage, just dying for somebody to take them out and bring them to life once more. When we showed Bob our plans for the cinema carriage, his eyes went all watery, he mumbled about his son in Albury, and asked would he get to travel on the train as projectionist.

'Bob, we'll name the cinema after you!' said Al. 'Bob's Trans-Continental Cinema. How do you like that? You and Ethel will have your own room modelled after the honeymoon suite on the Southern Aurora!'

I'm sure I saw Bob's face go slightly pink.

The cinema carriage would be a big drawcard for travellers sick of the recent re-run type entertainment they get on aeroplanes. We would show only old re-runs, the classics, and some cartoons and classroom-science short films from the fifties.

We would build a sloping floor in one of the baggage cars. Bob had a lot to do with this. 'What if you get seated behind a lady wearing a big hat with feathers?' It could happen, I suppose. We couldn't tilt the floor, as hard as we tried, so we built one end higher and set the seats out in semi-circle rows.

Bob had some bits he saved from the old Paramount cinema when they pulled the guts out. It nearly killed him to see that place destroyed, with its beaded glass hangings and the organist who would rise up mysteriously on a moving platform from within the stage. Ethel thought he had finally gone crazy when he arrived home with a truckload of red velvet cinema seats, but she didn't let on. She noticed how pale Bob's face had become.

Ethel said she'd let him keep the seats in the house. Bob just said, 'I can't look at those things all the time. You have to move on in life, Ethel. I think it's a shame to throw out such good seats, is all.' Often, when she went out to his shed to call him in for supper, Bob would be slumped asleep, his white hair fanning over the red velvet like a Chinese party decoration.

Our cinema screen wasn't as big as one at the movies nowadays, but it was big enough to see whether an actress's beauty spot was painted on.

The speakers were assorted out-takes from hi-fi systems. We set them around the carriage at two-metre intervals. Bob insisted that the projection table be fitted with the best suspension for his equipment, a Leica classic projector. Al took a conglomerate of parts from an old Citroen car. When you started the projector up, it tilted forward.

So we were progressing smoothly and refining our plans all the time. Every Saturday and Sunday we would be out in our yard, now as jumbled as the rest of the house. Even our neighbours wanted to be involved.

One family watched all the home renovation shows on television and took notes on topics they thought useful. They would pop these over the fence. Unfortunately, we didn't intend to stencil heritage designs on to stretch fabric, or make nifty faux-steel benchtops out of metallic paint and contact adhesive film. No, everything in our train was going to be what it purported to be!

Ethel was still wheedling for the job of chief cook. She made morning tea using the train's ancient kitchen, and served it in thick railway china. There were no biscuits or scones with the tea, she was working up to that. We sat in the armchairs of the outdoor scenery carriage, surveying our train. Ethel called the beverage 'depression coffee'.

Al did have to ask how it was made. 'Burnt bread crusts in hot water, dear. Like in the old days.' Hmmm. It certainly depressed me to hear that.

Before long, the train would be ready for its

maiden voyage. For publicity, we decided to run a competition for its name, in conjunction with the Melbourne Zoo who were running a competition to name their new baby gorilla. We could have the runner-up name, it was agreed, as long as the gorilla family had a carriage built for them to visit their relatives at the Taronga Zoo in Sydney. This sounded like a good deal, as we thought lots of people would like to travel with the gorillas.

One day we received a letter from an artist living in Germany who had heard of our train. He was an experimental electronic musician. He wanted to do a collaboration with us, recording the train sounds and mixing them to make music. But another artist had proposed to install a xylophone made of steel, fixed to the undercarriage, which would change pitch according to the terrain and resonate with the wheels on the tracks.

We said we were happy to invite musicians on board, and they were both welcome if they could sort out who would do what where and with what, and if, when it was the gorillas' bedtime, they would stop.

By now we had a lot of people interested in taking up residence on our train. Somebody from the national weather bureau turned up in our yard one day wanting to install a device free of charge that would monitor the temperature, relative humidity and wind direction as the train crossed the country. We didn't really need to know all those things as we would be experiencing them instead, but she said it was more for the people who needed constant weather updates.

The findings would be beamed to a satellite and down to Earth. I guess we could have said no then, but we felt sorry for those people without weather. The next week, a truck came to our yard with a huge transmitter on its back, big as a giant's teacup.

'Where are you going to put that?' Al asked the driver.

'It needs to go in an open space, so, let's see . . . right there.'

He was pointing to the fresh-air-and-scenery-carriage. It would really block the view.

'Are you sure you don't have a smaller one?'

'Sorry, but it needs to be a strong one to beam the weather into space.'

'Um, OK. But if it gets in the way too much it has to go.'

Great! Now we had an enormous high-technology passenger along with everybody else, which was making for a very full train:

the cinema in one baggage car;

the two musicians and their
equipment in another;

the fresh-air-and scenery carriage
with transmitter;

the vegetable garden carriage;

the guest gorillas in a passenger
carriage with straw on the floor;

Ethel and Bob in their suite (half a
carriage);

and me and Al in ours (the other
half).

There were two passenger carriages left
with a capacity of forty people, and a sleeper
carriage holding twelve. Bookings were start-
ing to come in by post for the first journey, and
the naming competition would be drawn that
month.

We still had the second dining carriage to fix
up. It was a remnant of a train from Darwin
that had been damaged by water during a
storm. Instead of restoring it, we made it into
a café-style eatery and games room where
people could sit at laminex tables and eat

sandwiches and play *Cluedo* and *Operation* and the board game from the hit movie, *Flashdance*.

Ethel's cooking was improving so much that we could almost trust her with food.

By now, the word had spread to the local schools. One school group came each week to paint a mural on the café carriage walls. It was like the 'history of transport' mural at Spencer Street Station only more colourful, and about fish and clouds. The teacher had a way of stirring up the kids' enthusiasm until they were frothing at the mouth to paint clouds. She told them to pretend they were angels and that every cloud they painted was like a present to somebody they loved and might never see again; she told them that each fish they painted would come alive in somebody's dream.

I don't know where she studied teaching exactly, but it really worked on those kids. They painted like they played in the sea.

The clouds-and-fish mural was so potent that every time I saw it, I was too overcome to eat my sandwiches and went into a rapture. Which was lucky: Ethel's sandwiches weren't too appetising.

Another school group came along to re-organise the coal stack. We had grey carpet to begin with anyway.

All these kids went home and told their parents they must take them on the train, which is why we had to double-and triple-book the passenger cars. They had helped so much, we felt we should give them priority. The train was already so full, but it was unlikely they would all turn up.

The gorilla-and-train-naming-contest was drawn, the name *Silver Cloud* going to the baby gorilla, leaving us with *Mr Ungly*.

We refused calls from all sorts of companies who wanted to sponsor us in return for advertising their soup or soap or soap-soup or whatever. A petrol company wanted us to endorse its brand of petrol. It didn't matter to them that we ran on coal. A toy company wanted to make fuzzy toy trains out of genuine kangaroo fur. We told them about our ultrasonic wildlife-warning device that played Waltzing Matilda at frequencies audible only to kangaroos, wallabies and other indigenous fauna. They asked could we play it backwards and attract the animals towards the train where they could be harvested for their pelts and sewed into cute fuzzy trains by outworkers in an on-board-slaughterhouse-tannery-and-sewing-factory? You can imagine what we said to that.

A film company called wanting to make a film about *Mr Ungly*, based in Los Angeles aboard a set costing two million dollars and starring John Travolta and whoever else was most marketable. I was feeling too tired to say no, but I had to. The train hadn't even been anywhere and already it was travelling out of our hands.

Al and I lay in bed that night, testing out our suite and wondering how it had come to involve so many people.

Our something-to-do-on-the-weekend had ballooned like a rampant virus into a circus of community involvement. It was too late to do anything but go with it, run the train for a year to Sydney and back, and then decide what to do.

The Grand Opening Day went, well, not exactly as planned but without loss of life.

We were seen off by television cameras and marching bands. A flock of doves, released into the air by a local club, were blackened by the coal smoke, but unharmed. Everybody aboard was squashed, but thrilled.

Mr Ungly travelled at 10 mph and made it to Seymour station by nightfall. The engine was about to explode with the strain. We all had to disembark and push the train into a siding. Suddenly most of the passengers hated us, we were *stupidly irresponsible* where before we'd been *fanciful visionaries*. The musicians were furious. The kids' parents were very sour at having to pick them up.

From then on, we said we'd not overfill the train, but few people wanted to go on the very slow train after that.

We became a club for Bob and Ethel's friends who liked to play cards and take their time, and our friends who felt sorry for us.

Only the gorillas were truly content with our pace. They made it to Sydney three days late but well-rested and having seen the landscape of Eastern Australia: endless fields of grass with the odd dried tree; paddocks full of hot sheep. They especially loved the part where, coming into Sydney from the mountains, you see only water each side of the train, like it's become a boat on wheels. They would talk about this for years. Yes, they were very, very contented gorillas.

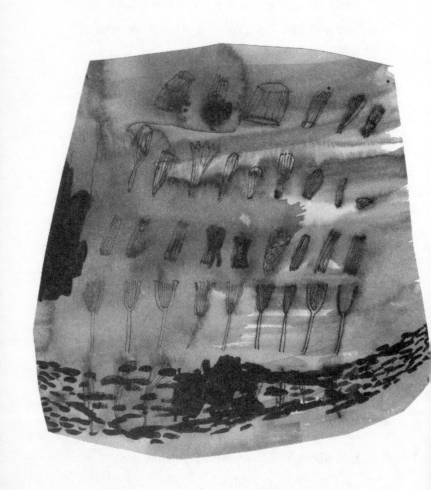

Syngamy

Dear Aunt Maudie,

How do I attract an insect pollinator?

I have tried everything from shimmying in breezes to singing love songs. I have studied ancient Greek, and am conversant with Geography. I can cook a mean quince pie. But I am afraid to die unfertilised, my stigma untouched by a single pollen grain, my carpel never growing into a fruit.

Please help me!

Yours longingly,
Melia.

Dear Melia,

It sounds, from your letter, as if you are a sophisticated young organism, but you seem to be a little misguided.

Insects are delicate creatures, and have specific desires and needs. Sadly, it doesn't matter how much you know of astronomy, and you can bake until the cowslips come home. An insect is after *one thing*.

Your task is to entice the insect towards your nectaries. Here's my advice:

 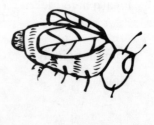

Make your flowers blue, white or purple. Hide them from unwanted birds, who prefer petals of conspicuous red. Colour them with carotenoids, if you can, so they glow alluringly in an insect's ultraviolet gaze.

An insect will search for miles for the bearer of a sweet scent! Make your flowers fragrant! Make the fragrance irresistible! Try a combination of high and low notes, citrus and musk. (Chanel No.5 is not advised.)

Make your flowers stand out pertly from your leaves. Make them rapturous! Make them intricate! Hold them up on stalks if you must.

Insects need to be guided and encouraged. They need to be shown the way with arrows! Make artful landing strips on your petals with ultraviolet pigments. An insect appreciates a comfortable landing platform.

Once the insect has arrived, keep still. Its feet will tickle, but try not to move. It will poke around your corolla before thrusting its proboscis deep into your gynoecium. During this climactic moment, you may be rewarded with a dusting of pollen grains upon your stigma. Provided the pollen is compatible, you will feel a pollen tube growing down your style.

You'll feel satisfied and mysterious. You'll want to offer the insect a cognac. But be warned, Melia! Insects don't drink spirits and they never stay for long. As soon as it takes your nectar, it's wiping its feet on your petals and taking off home.

Many organisms would say that grasses have it better; blowing clouds of pollen off into the wind, effortlessly gathering it up from another gust of air. Making small, plain flowers and not bothering about perfume. Doing without insect contact. None of this swelling up and losing your petals afterwards.

Personally, I think the sense of fulfilment that comes from that brief moment of ecstasy is worth every bit of trouble. And the anticipation is half the fun.

Yours in syngamy,
Aunt Maudie

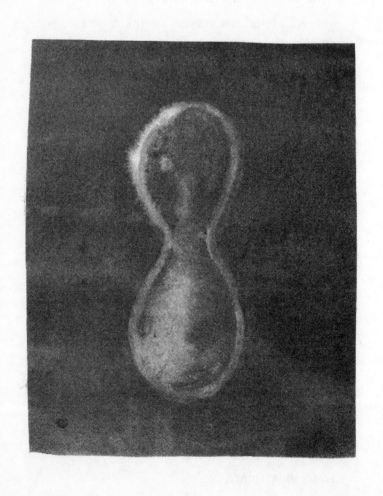

Bird Flying Upside-down

Fig.1 shows a picture of a glass bowl, buffed to evoke glass from the sea. Glass from the sea differs from ordinary glass, the way a plant dug up from a forest differs from a plant bought from a nursery. The glass bowl in the picture pretends to be glass from the sea but is actually not sea-worn, and when you hold it will say, 'What are you talking about?' if you ask it about the movement of water.

The glass bowl in the picture is one of many, made by a person who had no words left. He just took all his tired old words, compressed them under the weight of deadlines and work requirements and out came glass. Which surprised him. He was hoping for some new words that would lock together like meccano and inspire him to speak and write again. The bowls made him feel kind of happy. When he walked along the beach and a drizzle fell on his head, he would be thinking of his glass bowls; he could see them between his eyes and the wet, grey sand.

Fig.2 is a photograph taken in half-light, showing a collection of objects on a shelf. All the things share the colour aqua or are of a translucent material. One thing has both these qualities. It is a heavy glass egg, lying on its side, like sleeping. Next to the egg are some shells, all roughly the same shape, arranged in order from small to large. The largest looks to be about five centimetres long and two wide. Each shell has a small hole bored into it by one of those snails with the mouth on the end of a tube that go around in the sea tunnelling through other creatures' shells and sucking their bodies out the hole and down the tube and going away in search of their next victim.

Next there is a hen's egg that has come out more hourglass than ovoid, and another strange egg with a half-formed miniature egg accidentally moulded on the side. They have been preserved by having a pin-prick hole made in one end and the contents blown out. So there is a shaped space inside each egg, every surface curved.

Fig. 3 is a diagram of a room that has been made into a pinhole camera. A black covering has been taped to a window, and the door is closed and insulated with black tape. The only source of light is a tiny hole in the centre of the window-covering. The diagram conveys the mechanics of a pinhole camera in a simple way, with some arrows and clarifying words. The diagram was drawn with pen and ink and probably a ruler.

If this was a real room and you were standing in the middle of it, you would see everything that is outside the window projected onto the wall opposite, upside-down. If a bird flew by, you would see an image of it flying upside-down, inside the room, across the wall. But this is a diagram and you can only imagine the darkness and the lightness and the next-door neighbours' fence projected onto your lounge room wall.

Concerto for Autumn

Outside the front window this morning, a semi-improvised piece is playing: *Barry Street Concerto for Autumn*. The main instrument is a sea of cars on Westgarth Street washing in and out with the air current, which is the secondary instrument. The cars are tuned to play bass notes in the key of G. There is the occasional treble note sustained for a few seconds, fading into an exhalation by a tired old man waiting to cross the road. They play *pianissimo*, so softly you can hardly hear them when the sharp chirps begin in Section Two.

Sharp peeps, chirps and twitters. Chirrup, britt-britt, chit-chit-chit-chit coo-coo, chabree bree bree and wrhip are all played by geniuses who humbly spend their lives perfecting their instruments.

If you took a paper plate and folded it in

half six times and painted one wedge with going to bed early, and the wedge directly opposite, where the points meet, you painted with a new summer dress, you would have just made a map of the contrast between Section One and Section Two.

Woven around them in a complicated 7/15ths rhythm pattern are spoken-word performances. Highlights include: 'I got it started Thursday but since then it won't turn over,' and the poetic, 'Get in here and put your sandals on *noooow*!'

Section Two is punctuated by sudden door slams—house and car—that tell the listener there's more to Barry Street than contented comings and goings; there are also dramatic comings and goings. Various footfalls are heard, an electric saw, a motorbike.

Section Two features a white sky and a promising weather report.

Section Three displays the potential of surround stereo sound. From upstairs on the right comes a rumbling tantrum in 12/8 time that obscures all the other instruments. A whistle, and crash across the ocean of cars, a piping harmonic screech and it gets what it wants and thunders away to the left. It leaves you feeling as if you've just watched a child eat a whole chocolate cake made with twelve eggs and almonds and dirt.

Now to the crescendo. We hear echoes of the themes from Sections One and Two.

Mellow old dog barks are interspersed with coo-coo and the griping ring of a neighbour's phone. A gelati van chimes, every third note stolen by the air.

The soloist: a truck, taking a fast corner, scraping into the train bridge, stripping its left side of wood, exposing metal ribs.

Perhaps, if you took a rusted shed, filled it with old bones and had it shaken upside-down by sad zoo elephants, you would have an idea of the disturbing quality of the crescendo.

Barry Street Concerto for Autumn concludes with cheeps and twitters and the sky growing brighter. Still, a haunting feeling remains in the air. The cars trail off into silence.

The piece will be performed all of next week, the week after and the week after that, except for Easter, when it will tour the country.

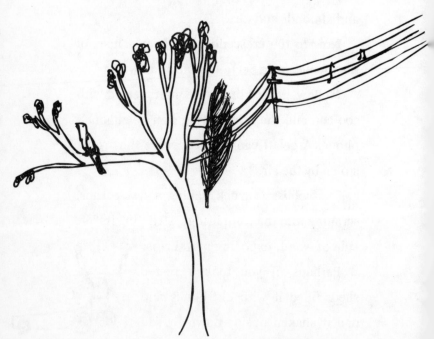

The CD Cover for Barry Street Concerto for Autumn

The CD cover for *Barry Street Concerto for Autumn* is a dark blue-and-white photograph of the way light comes in through a three-part window, where the two end parts are open to let the sound enter the room.

The photograph is grainy, to emphasise the light landing brightly on the inside of the right window frame, hitting and filtering through a dirty glass vase of scratchy flowers.

The image is printed on matt paper with *Barry Street Concerto for Autumn* in gloss raised letters, in an up-to-date font.

Although condensed from its original twelve-hour performance time, *Barry Street Concerto for Autumn*, the CD, faithfully reproduces the magic of live music, preserved for ever in crisp digital sound.

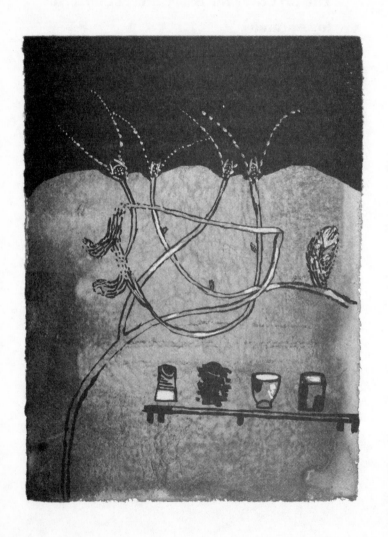

Best Left Alone

You know, sometimes, things happen that promise to make life breezy and blue, but turn out to make things more gluey and orange than before. I wish I'd thought that when Selwyn, the plant chemical salesman, came into the nursery last Thursday.

I was polishing the shiny-leafed bushes for the fourth time and struggling with writing my novel. I wrote it in a large notebook that I took everywhere with me. Polishing leaves helped me to think.

My novel was a fictionalised account of my grandfather's life, from the time he was found in a rubbish bin until he discovered his love of plants and started the nursery with plant cuttings he snipped from local parks.

I felt I was getting to the heart of my novel, after changing the plot-line every few days for most of the year, making Grandpa a Chinese refugee, a war hero, an Italian woman.

At last I had settled on telling Grandpa's story pretty much as he lived it, from the point of view of the old oak tree that stood outside the nursery.

Then came Selwyn.

Selwyn always walked in like he was an ambassador for Chem Tech. I'm sure he read the sales literature in bed, he was so keen. Come to think of it, he probably ate the company's products.

Maybe it was the spring air affecting him, but that day he was acting as if he had TOP SECRET written on his forehead. Like a teenage boy who's just had his first kiss and thinks nobody can tell.

'What have you got for us today, Selwyn?'

He glanced sideways. Looked over his shoulder. Swung his briefcase onto the counter, laid it flat, and unclicked the catches. It opened out like a concertina with samples inside, instead of music.

He pointed to each item in turn, singing persuasively in his nasally voice, 'Advanced plant products! Scientifically putting the range into orange and the pump into pumpkin!'

Among the lawn daisy poisons, pot ventilating sprays and weed mat shampoos was the standard selection of new-breed plant hormone formulas.

There's nothing unusual about that, in itself. These days, you can buy hormone washes to turn your roses red, hormone solutions to grow a lettuce in three days. There are even pellets to make elm trees grip onto their leaves in autumn.

'All I need today is some Rootit. Can I have two cartons?'

We use their root-promoting powder, to grow roots on stem cuttings, all the time at the nursery. It's much quicker than growing whole plants from seed.

He leaned across the acre of samples and cupped his hand around his mouth.

'Listen, Linda, you've been my best customer for years. Today I have something that will revolutionise your rooting routine. It's my personal formula. You'll to be the first to try it.'

No wonder he was looking cagey. If anybody from Chem Tech knew about this, he'd be in real trouble.

He took my hand in his and slipped me a ball of Easter-egg foil. He was whispering now. 'Inside this packet is enough rooting powder to turn every plant here into two hundred. This is very, very concentrated stuff. You only need to use . . .'

Just then, his watch beeped and he glanced at the window. A man in a dark suit walked into the shop and skirted the wall. Packing up his case, Selwyn mouthed something I couldn't make out. 'I'll be back Tuesday,' he said loudly, and imitated a person leaving a shop casually. I turned to greet the new customer in the suit, but he had vanished. That would be the last I saw of Selwyn.

The afternoon dragged on. There were a few sales, a run on cumquat trees. It was hard to concentrate with the powder burning a hole in my pocket. I knew I had to wait until everybody had left before I could unwrap the foil ball and try it out. So it was eight o'clock when I gathered some stems from around the nursery and went out to the greenhouse.

I thought I'd try it on the usual plants first, the easy-to-breed ones like begonias and geraniums. In the greenhouse at night, that's when this business comes to life for me. I sit at my potting bench under a bright lamp with my scalpel and formulas, like a surgeon, and I feel as if I'm seeing everything for the first time.

What Selwyn had told me about the powder made me sceptical. He was a professional exaggerator. He could call a slater bug a 'living fossil', and sell it to a museum. They'd have known it was a slater bug *before* Selwyn walked in, but afterwards, they'd have built it a special annexe.

I emptied the powder into a glass dish. It glimmered. There was about a tablespoon of it.

I dipped a few cuttings into water and dusted their ends with the powder. I stuck the cuttings of each type of plant into a separate pot of cuttings-mix soil, labelled them and put them on the warmed bench. Just as I have so many times.

If this stuff is so good, it should work on hard-to-propagate plants, I thought.

By the time I came back with an armful of magnolia branches, I realised just how strong it was. I should have put the powder back in its foil right then. *The cuttings I had just treated were now half-grown plants and were growing steadily while I watched in horror!* It was like a time-lapse film, but with no film. A geranium formed buds and flowers in seconds.

A chill went up my spine and a terrible mist filled my body. I felt the chill carry my mind upwards and out the top of my head. I watched myself act from a vantage point in the rafters. There was my body taking my half-finished novel from my bag; my arm, reaching over for a thirty-centimetre pot. There was my hand ripping out the pages of my notebook. It scooped soil over the only copy of my novel, watering it, mixing it into a mud pie with a magnolia branch, and sprinkling, then tipping, the rest of the powder into the pot.

My God, what was my body doing? I could only watch as my hands wrote a label and put the pot on the warmed bench.

What happened next, you may think is untrue, but I swear it's the worst thing I've ever seen. My novel started to sprout in white curls of paper from the black soil. It pushed upward rapidly. It became a smooth-barked treelet, reaching for the ceiling.

I saw everything as if it was covered by a white film. Next moment, I was waking from a faint on the damp nursery floor. Still, the tree-novel was growing at a hundred times the rate of a banana tree in Cairns.

My novel had grown into a magnolia tree, with myriad plot lines branching from the trunk. It made chapters of buds and was forming huge white flowers. Each petal had markings on it in the shape of sentences. My novel was growing so fast it was shedding leaves and petals over everything.

As I gathered the petals they began to wither, for just as they had grown in a matter of seconds, so they were fading before I could read the words.

I stood in the gloom of the greenhouse, beside wilted super-geraniums and begonias, holding my novel that was turning brown, my complete novel that I would never read.

Grandpa used to say, 'You can't improve on nature.' But I can imagine he would have made a fortune from all this, somehow.

A Dream, Displayed

One Saturday, one of those rainy afternoons when it could be night, you don't really know what the time is, I was wandering down a back street in town. This street had the feeling of tom cats and factories with signs that read 'back tomorrow'; it was that sort of lackadaisical street. If it even had a name, I couldn't tell you. And I did try to recall it, just the next day, when I wanted to return.

From out of the grey that was everything there appeared an arrow-shaped sign, red against the fence. Of course I followed it. In front there was another arrow pointing up a laneway, this one made of red pipe-cleaners twisted together. Then I saw the door.

Somebody had painted on it the words:

A Dream, Fabricated and Displayed

The lettering was a little creepy.

I felt like Alice in Wonderland, crawling through the doorway. Nothing much else was happening, that wintery Saturday.

On the other side of the door was a base-ment, in darkness, the floor bare bluestone decorated with damp patches and dirt. As my eyes adjusted, I saw that the walls were a combi-nation of crumbling red brick, salt-encrusted bluestone and mould-covered cement.

There were no windows and the entrance 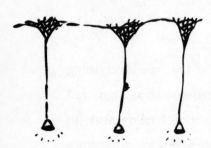 was the only way out. Small halogen lights were strung from the roof by cobwebs.

It smelled of the absence of air, and the presence of organisms that breathe in the shadows and live generations without seeing sunlight.

Stuck to the wall on my left was a sign with the words:

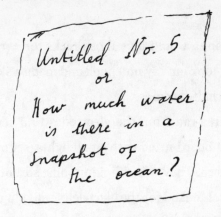

So it was an art exhibition. How funny, there was nobody there to mind it, and no name under the sign. There seemed to be some kind of life in the room, though. A kind of negative image of a page from a children's picture book: no flowers, no bears.

What I could only describe as a machine stretched along the left-hand wall of the room.

The machine comprised metal racks set into the bluestone wall, each rack cradling a glass preserving jar filled with a powdery ingredient and labelled in the same creepy writing: crushed fluorite, dirt, pulverised bone, grated plastic, rancid flour, each in suspension in a blueish fluid with a tiny electrode taped to the lid.

My nanna would love those racks for her jam jars. I took out my notebook and made a sketch in the half-darkness.

Wires ran from the electrodes to a central circuit board fitted with small lights, set out in a pattern. They were blinking some sort of language. I looked for the electricity wall plug, but there didn't seem to be one. It just ran off the power of what was in the jars. At that point, I stopped making drawings. It was like trying to draw love. Most of what matters about it is invisible and too hard to catch with a pen.

I was alone with this machine, and feeling a little scared, but anything was better than the emptiness I felt walking on the back street. I kept looking at the sculpture.

From that board of lights ran another spaghetti set of wires, leading to a metal arm. From the arm grew fingers of an old type-writer. Underneath, a conveyor belt carried pieces of a dismantled xylophone and flat metal cups of water. The typewriter fingers, activated by the wires, sometimes hit the xylophone keys, and sometimes the water. I felt a sense of hope within hopelessness.

Whoever made this sculpture must have had an instinct about mechanics. It seemed more like a living entity than a machine, as if it grew from an egg timer, nourished by radio music. My skin was tingling with excitement.

At the end of its revolution, the conveyor belt tipped out the water into a pool, from which a pipe, topped with a fountain, refilled the cups for it to start over.

The water pump was powered by a generator run on rotted teeth, rolled around in a kind of horrible 1950s mix master. The sound it made was as unnerving as watching an expensive Persian carpet being undone, strand by strand.

At the back of the basement was another machine. I liked this one the best. The sign on the wall said:

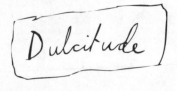

A super-8 projector shone a movie onto a fish tank filled with sugar-cubes and water.

The movie ran on a loop and showed an out-of-focus image of a cloud forming into a

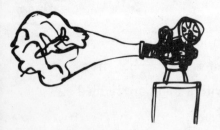

monster cloud and an aeroplane flying into it. The movie started again, repeated itself over and over.

The mixture in the fish tank was agitated by an air bubbler running on gas from a fermenting chamber, apparently topped up with contributions from interested members of the public. A printed notice stood next to it.

THE CHAMBER WILL ACCEPT:
dead flowers (particularly hospital bouquets)
jealousies   regrets (old and current)
soured milk and soy milk   chipped paint
toenails (don't have to be yours)
foul burps   parking tickets
IT WILL NOT ACCEPT:
letters of application   hard cover books
falafel balls   tissue paper from presents
staples   chewing gum (soft or hardened)

I stood there for a while, thinking about what I could put into the chamber. If I could have

worked out how to put regrets in, that would have powered it for a while, but soured milk seemed easier, and besides, I had some at home from my yoghurt project. I looked at everything one more time, and crawled back out into Saturday.

At home, I drew pictures all night and didn't answer the phone. I covered my table with incredible maps of the city. I drew charcoal roads that led down burrows and trees with birds on every branch. Something had been unravelled in me by seeing that exhibition.

I dreamed about what I would ask the person who had made the machine: 'Where did you start?' 'Did you carry it there?' But I also hoped nobody would be able to answer.

That room would be forever in my memory as a sublime and unexplained creation, and from there I could shape it into anything. The thought of that machine would fuel me through days of blank pages and rain.

So, it was Sunday when I went there again, to that same back street (well, it was the same area) and after hours of walking I thought I recognised the 'back later' signs and walked up the lane but there were no arrows and the sour milk was leaking.

The small doorway looked the same, exactly, so I pushed it open, expecting to hear the sound of whirring projector and ping of xylophone keys and roll roll crunch of rotted teeth.

Only dust floated out and I realised it was gone, whatever it was that had been there, and probably only cats slept there now, so I left them the milk.

Inventory Picture

Been thinking about a grey luscious painting with outlines of objects painted in while the paint is still wet. So there is a texture where the lines are traced. And it is about drawing and remembering these objects or the feelings they evoke. Not really about describing their form.

There's a picture I would give all my black sketchbooks, all my clay bowls, all my knitted animals to get back. It's an inventory of tools in grey-green and white oil paint. It was lost at a studio surprise clearance. That is, the owner of the building took our materials, stored pictures, bags of clay, hammers and screwdrivers and stretcher frames—things you wouldn't mistake for rubbish if you were a dog going through a skip bin—to the tip.

We found out a few weeks later. I always think you never regret seriously things you lose or toss out, and things you keep are probably better discarded. But this one picture lurks in my head. It embodies a feeling about painting that holds power for me and I'm worried is leaving. I try to paint it again, but I don't have the right space, the same size canvas, the same feeling. I feel if I could see that painting again I might be re-infected with the germ.

The thing about writing is that you have to know words to make sentences to talk about something. The thing about painting is that you don't think and translate. The thoughts go from the brain, down the arm (or foot, if you paint by foot), through the hand and come out in pure form. That's how it appears to me.

The memory of the grey-green picture is probably better than the actual grey-green picture. But I'm not convinced.

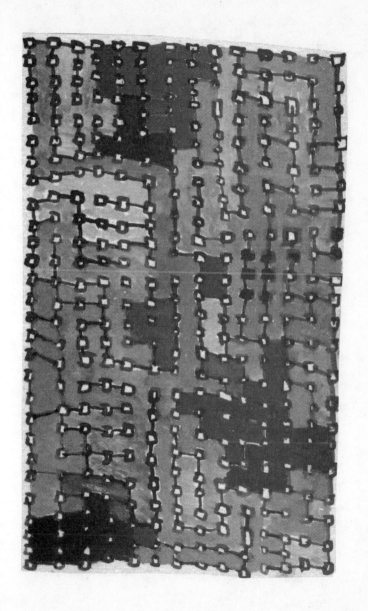

Amateur Investigator

I put things in a drawer to test whether it is true that things can only be seen when light shines on them. Including their colour, which some people would say is not innate, but is created, like a three-way tango between the object, the moon, and the eye of the beholder.

I am always neat about making records, in case I am made a professor and called upon to lecture in the future. Here is my first equation:

object + moon + viewer = coloured object.

I think it's something to do with the surface of the object, at a level we can't even imagine. It could be like tiny pebbles encrusted on it, or cracked glass. And depending on the texture, we see a colour. That's what I set out to examine, not what the surface looks like, but how it functions.

The drawer was made of precision mahogany and, once divested of socks, big enough to hold several test items at a time. I started out with yellow things, yellow being easy to see in low light. I took a banana, a tennis ball, and a toy canary, and labelled them with string and paper luggage tags. Because I wanted everything to be clear.

The side of the drawer had a hole drilled in, only as big as a worm. So I would be able to peek without letting light in. It was plugged with a piece of sterile cork.

The banana, the sock and the tennis ball were all new, bought from shops in the same block, on the same morning. They had to withstand rigorous testing.

Once the items were in the drawer, the scenario was sealed with a piece of tin tacked to the top, and replaced in the chest-of-drawers. I labelled the outside in case of interference.

Leaving it there to mature for a while, I set up the other drawer: one with varied colour items in it. I had a book with a green cloth cover, a red apple, three potatoes and a set of orange autumn leaves. All collected from different places at odd times.

I also sealed this drawer with tin, and labelled the outside. It had a similar viewing hole in the side. This drawer sat below the first, and above the undies.

I decided to leave the drawers for seven days before looking at them. This was incredibly difficult at first. I shuffled and reordered my index cards, sniffed at the cork stopper. Every time I was getting dressed the temptation would be there, and I had to think of how much better it would be to wait.

All was fine, until I started another experiment for the meantime, something to answer my questions about treasured objects:

Do ordinary things become infused with emotional ethers? From then on are they not plainly themselves but receptacles of moods? Are these signals interpreted by anyone, without thinking, like when you walk by the sea and feel the slow presence of starfish?

I became so carried away with this that I neglected the drawer test altogether. So I didn't look at it until two months later, when I'd become interested in sound waves and wanted the drawers for speaker boxes.

Anyway, I thought I'd better finish the experiment properly, so I carefully removed the cork and peered into the yellow drawer. I couldn't see a thing, but I could sure smell fermented banana. The coloured drawer was

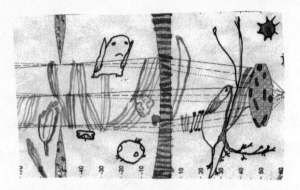

the same. Nothing. Maybe they had turned grey through being denied light. Whatever. I ripped the second drawer out of the cabinet and prised the tin off the top.

The pink apple was suffering from maggots, the autumn leaves were pale blue skeletons and the yellow cloth-covered book still looked boring. Only the potato had benefited from the holiday. Its tentacles filled the available space in the drawer like rainbow knitting, and were pushing out the cork.

I am sorry that nothing really came of the drawer test, but that's the life of an amateur investigator, trying one experiment and another, expecting to make sad discoveries.

Wonderful Shop

There is a wonderful shop off the main street.
You might know it—a big grey dog lies across
the doorway.

I walk past and
its never open
but I stand there
wishing it would
sell me something.

It sits in a street of vacant blocks, filled with
knee-high grass. That street seems always
bleached by sun; catching the afternoon and
stretching it out. The shop has tiles missing
and a ripped awning.

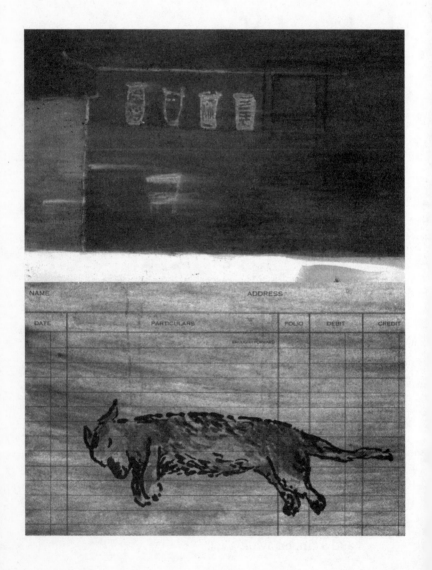

makes me think of
the pyramids
once covered in
green marble.

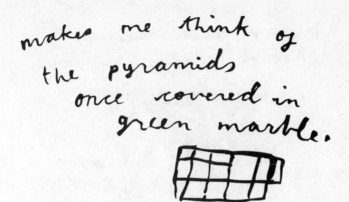

Coming across it is like accidentally finding a 1920s jazz station while turning off the radio.

Its specialty is little things in watermelon jars, ordered in an old-man-logic kind of way:

curled-up photographs next to
mixed buttons,
galvanised nails nudging tortoiseshell combs,
dog-biscuits beside fairground gonks.

I stand there peering
through the dirty window

I run my eyes along the shelves, **skipping**
over my favourite things, saving **them until**
last: the jar full of gravel, the jar **of bird**
feathers, the jar of pink air.

The brushy grey dog sleep-woofs, **his mouth**
closed, ears twitching.

I daydream that
I'm standing inside the shop,
pointing out my choice
from the array of jars.

Dust swims in the light struggling through the shelves. The light is losing the battle for colours. Anything not brown, black or grey has been sent outside.

I dream up a crumpled shopkeeper. He shuffles to the window, hitches up his apron, and climbs a wooden stepladder. He carries the jar of gravel like a precious walrus to a bench covered in newspaper and a big set of scales.

Would I like a box or a small jar? And how much gravel will that be?

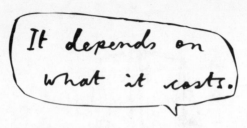

It depends on what it costs.

In my imagination, I always have a pocketful of notes.

He looks at me and I see he's not so old in the eyes. *Things here aren't for money,* he says. *You can take a piece of gravel home as long as you promise to look after it and keep it with you.*

I'm not too sure I can do that, I tell him. I don't want to feel eternally responsible for gravel. *How about the bird feathers?*

No, you don't look solid enough to take bird feathers. Come back for them in two years, I'll save you a couple. The only thing I can sell you today, then, is some pink air.

Great! I want to see him transfer it to a small bag the way they do with goldfish.

 This pink air was collected from the sunset on the night I was married, forty years ago. You intend to use it for your engagement, don't you?

Well, I don't know anybody, I say. Not even in my daydream.

In that case, there's nothing here for you today. Come back for the feathers. He picks out two seagull feathers, wraps them in newspaper, puts them under the counter.

There's no question of choosing from the other jars; this is not the kind of daydream shopkeeper you can disagree with. I feel the dust closing around me as he opens the door for me to leave.

I step across the big grey doorway dog, stirring from his sleep.

He stretches, groans and stares up at me.

His eyes are like holes through rainclouds in that perpetual afternoon outside the wonderful shop.

Before I go, I look along the rows of jars again. I notice a funny thing. The only jar half-empty is the jar of dog biscuits.

1998
2701

Topography of Wishes

Yesterday I went out to the back yard in the morning and fell over a mountain.

I don't know how it came to be there. It certainly was not there in the days before. It was made entirely of my discarded intentions, like half-ripe fruits fallen in a storm, rotting there in a heap. Some past hopes stuck to my shoe. They were typed out on slips of paper, screwed up tight. I don't know who typed them.

I picked some from the side of the mountain, unravelled them. They read:

`Learn to speak French and Italian.`
`Build high-rise beehive. Learn to oxyweld.`

Some ideas re-appeared several times:

`Oxyweld. Think about learning to oxyweld.`
`Weld up high-rise beehive.`

Plucking more papers from the mountain, I felt relieved that I hadn't done all these

projects. Otherwise there would be another
huge pile—of things—in the yard.

As I turned to walk inside, I saw, through
some missing fence palings, a pile of past
ambitions almost as tall as the neighbours'
roof. I was dying to read their mountain.

There was nobody around, so I climbed
through and took a piece from the north-
west face.

`Learn to swim.` (I can relate to that.) `Learn to
play guitar.` (Yep.) `Buy the kids a pony. Draw
a picture every day`. (Well, I guess everybody
thinks that.)

These were so fascinating that I kept reading: `Oxywelding workshop.` (Sounds familiar.)

Take dog to park before work. (Hang on, my dog is the only one in the street!)

I heard a noise and crept back to my own yard.

I scaled the roof of my house to see whether this phenomenon had affected the whole neighbourhood. From up there I could see white papery piles in other yards. The scene looked like a plaster relief map, white slopes shining in the morning sun.

I sat looking at the streets and buildings transformed by this topography of wishes. Behind the old folks' home rose a voluminous mountain range. Cars driving to work along the main road were held up by sad commuter fantasies.

In some yards the mounds were only small. Did these people never dream things up? Or maybe they dreamed realistic valleys; things they could finish.

Some piles were spread out, crushing bushes and small trees. Some were drowned, soggy in fish ponds. Others making their way indoors.

Just then a breeze picked up. I saw it coming from the west, lifting the slips of crumpled paper from their piles, carrying them like a flock of crippled origami birds over fences and rooftops, depositing them in trees, gutters and on other piles, mixing up people's old ideas.

I guess most of them will end up in the Maribyrnong River and block it.

Mechamarina

Saturday night. We were in the bath again, where many great scientific advances have taken place. But not tonight. The candlelight made the room into a cabin, cosy, as if nothing outside existed.

We started off talking about what sort of house we would build if we could, and ended up at a discussion about the Internet and why it sucks and how he's waiting for the bubble of computer art to burst. We wandered around the way wood feels better than expanding foam as a building material, clambered over why you

shouldn't pick up your dog's poo, and skirted a hypothesis on the contribution of the automatic gas hot-water service to the lack of real wood-chopping-type meaning in people's lives, when I realised we were only speaking for ourselves on that point.

'Not having an open fire is making me miserable,' I said, 'and drying wet clothes with a hair dryer is not the same.' Then one of the candles went out in sympathy with the tepid bath water. People of the future will probably feel sorry for us not having a bath water additive that keeps it hot.

A breeze whispered through the glass lattice window and I heard the voice of my Grandma Leah explaining to me-as-a-child the parts of her silver butter cooler, shaped like a globe with a sliding hemisphere, so smoothly machined and engraved with a twisting ivy vine. I would pretend it was a domed roof, over a miniature city, that opened for the sun and closed for the rain.

So I'm at my table now, looking in my Victorian Catalogue of Household Goods for an engraving of a butter cooler, when I remember an incredible item in the category of Mechanically-Moving Figures, Windmill, etc. With Music. The description that goes with the engraving follows:

No.6667.- Mechanical piece, under glass shade with canopy of flowers, representing a monkey nurse with baby. The nurse is dressed in blue and red satin, with white apron and

white lace cap, and is apparently feeding
the baby with a feeding bottle. Two airs of
music. Height 26 inches, length 20 inches.

I look at the picture and wonder: did these
things actually exist? Is this how people amused
themselves before television was invented? Did
families sit together after dinner and watch the
monkey?

Recently, I've been trying to understand Archimedes' principle about water and mass and volume. First I have to stop thinking that mass means size, as in: I saw a massive leopard slug in the dog's food bowl.

After a late dinner last Wednesday, when I was peacefully staring at the wall shadows made by the string lampshade, R stood up and said, 'I'm going to do an experiment to demonstrate our principle of the month.' He returned from the kitchen carrying:

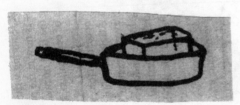
a frying pan with a lunchbox full of water sitting in it

a plastic bag

a reserve glass of water

a tomato

and a chopstick.

'I'm going to prove that the weight of the volume of water displaced by my sinking the tomato is equal to that of the tomato.' He held the tomato aloft.

'If this tomato floats, I'm going to poke it down and submerge it.' (Sticking the chopstick in one end of the tomato.) 'Then the water that spills over the edge of the lunchbox will be collected in the frypan and weighed. Oh shit! How did that water get into the frying pan?' There's a crack in the lunchbox.

I resume staring at the wall shadows while he rummages in the lab for a substitute.

Continuing the experiment, he pours water up to the rim of the new lunchbox. He lowers the tomato on a stick into the water. The tomato slides gracefully off the stick.

Well, we had to set up the experiment again and this time it stayed on its stick and I assisted to pour the water from the pan into the plastic bag for precision weighing by holding the tomato in one hand and the bag in the other and closing our eyes.

'So if the water was heavier, the tomato would float, but, as it weighs the same or more, it sank.'

By this time I am really tired and confused by the terms being used. I'm nodding. I know he can tell my brain is inert. Like the tomato, prodded and floated in the lunchbox, far from its origins. I feel I am a nodding monkey mechanically replicating the motion of an intelligent person. I watch his long fingers waving in front of me and squint as if he's drawing an invisible, glowing plan in the darkened air.

When I go to bed that night, I close my eyes

to see an open Victorian catalogue book, big as a blanket, hovering above my head. The words on the page scroll up as film credits do, only blurred like under water. I look at the wavering pictures and can just make out the words:

Mechanical piece under glass shade representing a dwelling constructed from expanding foam, where the bathroom comprises much of the living area. Two monkey figures, richly dressed in polyester, stick fruit with eating utensils and open their eyelids as if in conversation. The manner in which they prod the fruit is very serious. Two airs of music. Height 24 inches, width 22 inches.

About the Author

Trudy White lives in Melbourne, near the Merri Creek, where she spends too much time in the garden. She has studied painting, beekeeping, plant science and writing. She now paints, writes, edits and works in a Chinese herb dispensary. Her favourite books are picture books and old nature encyclopedias with hard covers and detailed engravings.